ADVENTURES IN THACKERVILLE

ADVENTURES IN THACKERVILLE

Steven R. Thacker

authorHOUSE®

AuthorHouse™
1663 Liberty Drive
Bloomington, IN 47403
www.authorhouse.com
Phone: 1-800-839-8640

© 2011 by Steven R. Thacker. All rights reserved.

No part of this book may be reproduced, stored in a retrieval system, or transmitted by any means without the written permission of the author.

First published by AuthorHouse 10/19/2011

ISBN: 9781467043151 (sc)
ISBN: 9781467043144 (ebk)

Library of Congress Control Number: 2011917618

Printed in the United States of America

Any people depicted in stock imagery provided by Thinkstock are models, and such images are being used for illustrative purposes only.
Certain stock imagery © Thinkstock.

This book is printed on acid-free paper.

Because of the dynamic nature of the Internet, any web addresses or links contained in this book may have changed since publication and may no longer be valid. The views expressed in this work are solely those of the author and do not necessarily reflect the views of the publisher, and the publisher hereby disclaims any responsibility for them.

Dedication

This book is dedicated to my precious wife, Debby Jo, and our three sons, Corey, Shawn, and Cody, our daughters-in-law, April and Esther and to our seven precious Grandchildren—Courtney, Candace, Cassandra, Cameron, Chelsea, Halle and Sarah. They are the joy of my life. A special thanks to my wife, our son Shawn and his wonderful wife Esther who so graciously did the editing of this material. Steven R. Thacker

CHAPTER 1

ADVENTURES IN NATURE

"It's Broken"

Once upon a sunny day in Thackerville, *where it is never right to do wrong and it is never wrong to do right*, a little girl was confused.

One day, while looking at Mommy's flower garden, Courtney saw a strange thing.

She saw a little worm moving in the oddest way. He would move his back legs forward while his front legs stayed still, then his back legs stayed still while his front legs moved forward. She ran in to tell her Mommy.

"Mommy, Mommy!" she shouted as she came into the house.

"What is it?" ask Mommy.

"I just saw a funny little worm in your flower garden and I think that he is broken."

"Broken?" Mommy asked with a puzzled look on her face.

"Yes, Mommy, come and see!"

Courtney took Mommy by the hand and led her outside to the flower garden to show her the 'broken' worm. "See, Mommy," said Courtney, "he's broken."

"No, he's not broken," said Mommy happily, "he is an inchworm."

"What is an inchworm Mommy?" asked Courtney.

She became thoughtful for a moment, "Does he measure your garden?"

"No," said Mommy, "we only call them that because of the strange way that they move along the ground. It looks like he is measuring the ground as he crawls along."

"Oh, I see," said Courtney, "God designed him in a special way, didn't He Mommy?"

"Yes, He did, Courtney," Mommy said with a smile.

"Only God could make something as special as an inchworm."

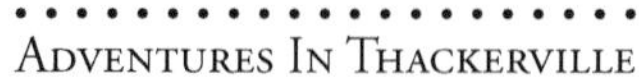

Grandma's Toy

Once upon a sunny day in Thackerville, *where it is never right to do wrong and it is never wrong to do right*, two little boys learned a secret from their Great Grandma, Cora Weaver.

One day Corey and Shawn took a journey with their parents to their Great Grandma Weaver's home near Portsmouth, Ohio.

"How old is Grandma Weaver?" ask Corey.

"Well, she is 95 this year," said Daddy with a smile. "We always love to come for a visit, don't we boys?"

"Yes, we do!" said Shawn, "she always has great stories to tell."

"I would love to go down over the hill to see the big rocks and caves where Daddy played when he was a kid," Corey said.

"Well," said Mommy, "we're here."

As they got out of the car, they saw Grandma standing on the front porch with her apron on and her bonnet on her head.

"Hey, kids!" Grandma shouted, "I have something to show you."

"What is it?" Shawn wondered in amazement.

"First," she said, "go to my garden, and get me two corn stalks."

"Okay!" they both said, as they raced to the garden. Soon they were back and standing in front of Grandma on her porch, with the cornstalks in hand.

"Here they are," said Corey, "but why do you need them?"

"You'll see," said Grandma as she took the corn stalks, cut them to about two feet long, and placed a small notch in one end. She picked up a small stone and placed it into the notch.

Then, with a quick flick of her wrist, the rock whistled into the woods.

"Wow!" shouted Shawn. "Corey, did you see that?"

"I sure did!" said Corey excitedly.

Then they ran off to play with their new toys.

....

Steven R. Thacker

A Bug with Racing Stripes

Once upon a sunny day in Thackerville, *where it is never right to do wrong and it is never wrong to go right*, a little boy and his sister saw a strange bug.

As Cameron journeyed around his house near his Momma's flower garden, he saw a 'funny' looking little bug with little black stripes flying from flower to flower. He quickly ran into the house to find his Mommy.

"Mommy, Mommy!" he shouted, "come and see!"

"What's wrong?" Mommy asked.

"I saw a funny little bug with racing stripes flying around your flowers," he said.

"Racing stripes?" she questioned.

"Oh," laughed Mother. "I understand."

"Don't touch it!" Mommy warned, "it's a bee and it might sting you. He is gathering sweet nectar for his family from the flowers. You may go and watch him, but stay at a safe distance."

"I will," said Cameron.

He went back outside with his sister, Chelsea, and watched at a safe distance, as Mommy had warned him, until the bee finally flew away to his family.

"I like bees," said Chelsea, "they are just like Daddy."

"How are they like Daddy?" wondered Cameron.

"Because they work hard all day to feed their family, too," explained Chelsea.

"Yes, and I really like their racing stripes," said Cameron.

The Beautiful Blanket

Once upon a sunny day in Thackerville, *where it is never right to do wrong and it is never wrong to do right,* a little girl was frightened.

One day Chelsea went outside to play with her brother, Cameron. As they walked under the little apple tree, they saw a large bug with long legs.

Chelsea ran to her Daddy who was working in his garage. Chelsea shouted, "Daddy, Daddy, there is a big long-legged bug under the apple tree!"

"Oh," said Daddy, "that would be a spider. If you don't bother her, tomorrow morning you will see a wonderful sight. She will make a web that will look like a beautiful blanket. It is one of God's little miracles."

The next morning Chelsea rushed outside with her brother, Cameron, to look for the miracle under the apple tree.

There sparkling with dew was a beautiful web stretched out like a beautiful blanket just as her Daddy had said.

"Daddy was right," said Chelsea.

"About what?" Cameron asked.

"This web looks like a beautiful blanket," she said. "It must be one of God's little miracles."

The Little Green Bags

Once upon a sunny day in Thackerville, *where it is never right to do wrong and where it is never wrong to do right*, two little girls went out to play.

One morning after breakfast Halle and Sarah went outside to go and play on their play set that their Daddy had built for them. On their way out the door they saw a strange sight. On the porch railing were hanging five little green bags. They ran back inside to tell Mommy what they had found.

"Mommy, Mommy!" they shouted, "come and see the little green bags."

Mommy ran to the door and looked at the bags. "Oh," she said, "these are cocoons."

"What are cocoons?" ask Halle.

"They are little worms that have enclosed themselves in these little green bags and later they will come out looking very different," Mommy said.

"Different how?" ask Sarah.

"You will see," said Mother with a smile on her face. "You just keep watching them and you will see a beautiful wonder of God's design."

Every day the two little girls went out on the porch to see the little green bags. One morning they noticed that one of the little green bags was open. Halle ran into the house and shouted, "The bag is broken, Daddy, the bag is broken!"

Her Daddy took the girls by the hand and walked them out onto the porch. "Look over here on Mommy's flowers," Daddy said, "this is what came out of the little green bag."

There on the flowers they saw a beautiful little yellow butterfly.

"It is a wonder in God's design, like Mommy said." said Halle.

Halle and Sarah were amazed each day as they saw the little green bags open one by one and reveal another little yellow butterfly - God's little miracles.

The Moving Rock

Once upon a sunny day in Thackerville, *where it is never right to do wrong and it is never wrong to do right*, two little girls discovered a mysterious rock.

One bright morning, as they were playing in their playground, Cassie and Candy noticed a strange little rock.

"Look at this!" shouted Candy.

Cassie came running over to her from the slide, her favorite part of the playground.

"What is it?" she asked.

"It is a funny little rock," Candy said. "Maybe it rolled down from the woods on the hill."

"I know," said Candy, "we'll put it over here by the garage in Mommy's flower bed."

"Okay," said Cassie.

Just then, Mommy called for them to come for lunch. They ran inside the house and washed their hands very well because they had been playing in their playground.

After lunch they rushed back outside to play in their playground again. When they got to the playground, they noticed that the little rock was back.

"Mommy, Mommy!" they shouted, "come and see."

Mommy looked at the little rock and said with a smile, "Oh, I see girls. This is not a rock. It is a turtle. He must like your playground."

The girls named the little turtle 'Rocky' and they kept him in their playground. Cassie thought that his favorite part was the slide just like her.

The Fuzzy Worm

Once upon a sunny day in Thackerville, *where it is never right to do wrong and it is never wrong to do right,* a little boy saw a strange thing.

One Sunday afternoon, as he returned home with Daddy and Mommy from church, Cody saw a strange little worm on a leaf by their back door.

"Look, Daddy," said Cody, "look at this fuzzy little worm."

"I see him," said Daddy, "he is a caterpillar. Do you remember last year on Halle and Sarah's back porch there were some little green bags that contained little yellow butterflies?"

"Yes, I remember that," said Cody.

"Well," said Daddy, "this is the little worm that makes those little green bags and it turns into that beautiful butterfly. It is one of God's little miracles. This little worm eats leaves for food."

"He doesn't look much like a butterfly right now," said Cody.

"What a wonderful miracle of God's design," said Daddy. "He begins life crawling on the ground, and later, he flies through the air.

Only God can make a caterpillar to change and have a new life as a butterfly."

Grandma's Little Baskets

Once upon a sunny day in Thackerville, *where it is never right to do wrong and it is never wrong to do right,* Grandma made a little basket.

One day ten little children had gathered at Great Grandma Weaver's house. She called them down to the 'Old Oak Tree'.

"Come here, children," she called.

As they gathered around, she picked up a little acorn that was on the ground. With a small knife she began to carve the little acorn. As Grandma carved she told a story.

"This big oak tree was not always so big," she said. "It was once a little acorn just as you are little boys and girls. After a long, long time, as it stood its ground and was faithful to its' Creator, it grew and grew. As it got bigger it dropped little blessings like these little acorns. This little acorn can do three things."

"What?" the children asked.

"Well," Grandma continued, "it can feed God's little creatures like the squirrels, it can be the seed for more trees, or it can give a little gift to children like you."

Then she showed them a little basket that she had carved from the acorn.

"God wants you to be a blessing to others all through your life," Grandma said. "As the 'Old Oak Tree' you should also stand your ground and be faithful to your Creator."

Then, one by one, she showed them how to make a basket from the little acorn, just as she had done.

Tickling Fishing Worms

Once upon a sunny day in Thackerville, *where it is never right to do wrong and it is never wrong to do right*, two little boys were shown how to tickle a worm.

One night, as they were playing outside, Shawn and Corey noticed their Daddy in the back yard. He was bent over with a flashlight looking for something. They ran inside the house and told Mommy what they had seen.

"Do you think that Daddy has lost something and we should go help him find it?" asked Corey.

"Well," said Mommy, "I guess we could go ask him."

So, Corey, Shawn, and Mommy ran outside and shouted, "Daddy, do you need some help?"

"No," said Daddy in a low voice, "I'm just tickling worms out of the ground, and you must be very quiet or they will go back down into the ground." "Would you like to help?" he whispered.

"We sure would!" said Shawn quietly. "What do we do?"

"When the ground is wet from a fresh rain," Daddy explained, "the fishing worms come to the surface, but if you are not careful, when you grab them, they will quickly go back down into the ground. So, you need to take your finger and rub their side and tickle them while you gently pull them out with the other hand."

The excited little boys pulled the fishing worms out one by one and placed them into a bucket that Daddy had provided.

"Tickling really works," said Shawn.

"It sure does," Corey whispered, "but you have to be very quiet."

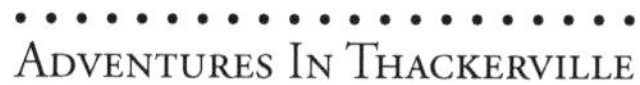

The "Buzzing" Bees

Once upon a sunny day in Thackerville, *where it is never right to do wrong and it is never wrong to do right,* two little girls heard a strange noise.

One morning, as they went outside to the garden shed to look for their soccer ball, Courtney and Chelsea heard a strange buzzing sound. "What is that noise?" asked Chelsea.

"I don't know," said Courtney, "it wasn't buzzing when we first came in here."

"It sounds like Mommy's buzzer on the stove when she is baking cookies, but the cookies are done." Chelsea said.

"Well," said Courtney, "I don't think that Mommy is baking any cookies in this garden shed. Let's get out of here!"

So, the girls ran as fast as they could to find Daddy.

"Daddy, Daddy!" the girls shouted all out of breath.

"What is the matter?" Daddy questioned.

"There is a burglar in the garden shed!" Chelsea shouted.

"Yes," said Courtney, "and he has a buzzer.

"A burglar with a buzzer," chuckled Daddy.

So, the girls took their Daddy back to the garden shed. Once there Daddy went inside alone and returned quickly.

"Well, Daddy, did you find him?" ask the girls.

"I didn't find him," said Daddy, "but I did find them. There is a nest of a thousand bees by the sound of them."

"Tonight I will come back while they are sleeping and spray them. Please stay away from here, okay, girls?"

"Okay!" said the girls.

So, the next day all was well just as Daddy had promised.

CHAPTER 2

ADVENTURES IN THE BACKYARD

The Ground is Moving

Once upon a sunny day in Thackerville, *where it is never right to do wrong and it is never wrong to do right,* two little girls saw a strange thing.

One morning, as she went outside with her sister, Sarah, to play, Halle noticed that the ground was mound up and the mound went across the yard. As she looked closer, she noticed that the mound was moving. She ran inside to tell her Daddy about the moving ground.

"Daddy, Daddy!" she shouted, "come and see the moving ground. We are having an earthquake!"

"Earthquake?" Daddy asks. "Yes," said Halle, "my Sunday school teacher told us of how the earth quaked and the ground moved when Jesus was crucified, and the ground in our backyard is moving. Come and see."

So, Daddy took the excited little girls by the hand and went to the backyard, and sure enough, the little mound was moving. "Oh!" exclaimed Daddy, "I see what you mean. However, this is not an earthquake. It is a little burrowing animal called a mole. He tunnels under the ground looking for little worms called grubs. We must get this mole to leave our yard."

"How do you do that, Daddy?" Halle asked.

"If we get rid of the grubs the mole will leave," said Daddy. "I have something to spread on the lawn that will get rid of them."

"Can we help?" ask Sarah.

"No!" said Daddy. "The little pellets that I must use could hurt you, so you must stay at a safe distance. Okay?"

"Okay," said the girls.

So, after a few days, when Daddy said it was safe, the girls were allowed to play outside again. They noticed that the ground had stopped moving. Just like Daddy had said.

The "Eperbemic"

Once upon a sunny day in Thackerville, *where it is never right to do wrong and it is never wrong to do right,* a little girl saw (in her words) an 'eperbemic'.

Chelsea, being sick for several days with the chicken pox and unable to play with the other children, was finally allowed to venture outside. She felt well enough this day to go outside for a little sunshine. As she walked around the yard, she notices a group of little bugs with spots on their backs. She ran into the house and reported to her Mommy that there was an "eperbemic" outside.

"What did you say?" Mommy asked.

"There is an 'eperbemic' outside, Mommy!" Chelsea said excitedly.

"What is an 'eperbemic', Chelsea?" Mommy asked.

"Our teacher at Sunday school said that when a lot of people have the same sickness then it is an 'eperbemic'."

"Oh, you mean an epidemic."

"Yes, Mommy, and there is a big one outside!" Chelsea said excitedly.

So, Mommy took Chelsea by the hand and went to see this strange sickness.

"Oh, I see, Chelsea," Mommy said with a smile, "these little bugs are called lady bugs. They are supposed to look like that. That is the way God made them."

"Goodie," said Chelsea with a sigh of relief, "we don't need any more chicken pox around here."

The Rude Worm

Once upon a sunny day in Thackerville, *where it is never right to do wrong and it is never wrong to do right,* a little boy was insulted.

One day Courtney went outside to find Cameron. She looked and she looked and finally found him in the backyard lying on his stomach and staring intently under the woodpile.

"What are you looking at, Cameron?" Courtney asked.

"I'm looking at a very, very rude worm," he said.

"What makes you think that the worm is rude?" questioned Courtney.

"Because he is sticking his tongue out at me," he answered.

"I'll go get Daddy," said Courtney. She ran into the house to tell Daddy what was going on.

Daddy ran outside quickly. "Cameron, Cameron," Daddy shouted, "move away from that woodpile!"

"Okay," Cameron said, "but why Daddy?"

Daddy went over to Cameron, picked him up, and walked carefully away from the woodpile.

"That was not a rude worm under that woodpile," Daddy said. "It was a snake. The snake sticks its tongue out to catch small, little bugs in the air and not to be rude."

"Can I keep him for my pet?" Cameron pleads.

"No, son," Daddy warned, "he is quite content in the woodpile with his family and he may get frightened of you and bite you. So please stay away from the woodpile."

"Okay, Daddy," Cameron said, "but I'm glad that he was hungry and not rude."

Bubbles in the Sky

Once upon a sunny day in Thackerville, *where it is never right to do wrong and it is never wrong to do right,* a little girl saw bubbles.

Courtney was outside in her playground. As she started to climb up the ladder to the slide, she looked up and saw all kinds of bubbles in the sky. They were all the colors of the rainbow. She ran into the house to tell Mommy.

"Mommy, Mommy!" she shouted.

"What is it, Courtney?" Mommy asked.

"The sky is full of bubbles!" she said excitedly. "Come and see."

So, Courtney and her Mother ran outside to see what Courtney was so excited about. There in the sky were dozens of hot air balloons.

"Those are called hot air balloons," Mommy said. "Aren't they beautiful?"

"Yes, Mommy, they are," said Courtney with a smile on her face.

"I have an idea," Mommy said, "wait here."

She hurried into the house. A few minutes later she returned with a blanket and a picnic lunch.

"We will have a picnic here in the backyard and watch them."

"Oh, yes, Mommy," Courtney said, "that's a great idea."

So, they ate their lunch and enjoyed watching the balloons until they had all floated out of sight.

Someone is Knocking

Once upon a sunny day in Thackerville, *where it is never right to do wrong and it is never wrong to do right,* a little boy heard somebody knocking.

One sunny morning, as he was playing in his back yard, Cody kept hearing someone knocking. He ran over to the shed and listened but the knocking was not coming from the shed. Then he hurried to the garage and listened; the knocking was not coming from the garage. He rushed into the house and asked his Daddy to help him solve the mystery of the strange knocking.

As Cody and his Daddy went outside they listened carefully for the knocking and soon they heard it.

Knock - knock - knock went the sound. Knock - knock -knock.

"Did you hear that, Daddy?" Cody wondered.

"Yes, I did," replied his Daddy, "come over here."

He took Cody by the hand and led him to a big oak tree at the back corner of their yard.

"Look up there on that big limb to the left," Daddy said as he pointed up into the tree.

"Oh, I see!" said Cody excitedly.

Then Cody became thoughtful for a moment, "What is it?"

"It's a woodpecker," Daddy said. "He has been designed in a very special way by his Creator to be able to tap little holes in the tree with his beak to get bugs to eat."

"Doesn't that give him a headache?" questioned Cody.

"No," said his Daddy with a giggle, "but it does look painful doesn't it?"

"It sure does!" said Cody, "it sure does."

Something is Wrong!

Once upon a sunny day in Thackerville *where it is never right to do wrong and it is never wrong to do right,* a little girl tried to surprise her Mommy and Daddy—and she did!

One morning Sarah decided that she would surprise her Mommy and Daddy by dressing herself. She was oh so very quiet. First she pulled on her favorite yellow shirt and then she pulled on her blue slacks. She put on her socks with lace on the top and then her black shiny shoes just like Mommy would usually do for her.

She was so happy with herself. "Daddy, Mommy, look at me," she shouted as she ran into the kitchen to surprise them.

As she entered the room all eyes were fixed on little Sarah. There she stood with her pants on backwards and her shoes on the wrong feet and the shirt was on wrong side out.

Mommy looked at Daddy and said with a slight grin, "Well, Daddy, what do you think of our big girl this morning?"

Daddy said kindly, "I think with a few changes she would look just fine."

God does not expect us to be perfect, but He does expect us to make an effort.

Sarah was a good girl. She wasn't perfect but she had made an effort and that is what is really important.

THE "SLIPPERY" DUO

Once upon a sunny day in Thackerville, *where it is never right to do wrong and it is never wrong to do right*, two little girls were caught in a slippery situation.

One evening, just before bedtime, Daddy and Mommy were enjoying a quiet evening in the living room when, all at once, they heard a little noise. Daddy looked over at Mother and she had a strange look on her face.

"What's wrong?" Daddy asked.

"I just realized that our two little look-a-likes are strangely quiet," she whispered.

"We had better look for them quickly and quietly," said Daddy as they crept toward the sound of some noise coming from the kitchen. As they peeked around the corner, they saw the twins sitting in the middle of the kitchen floor, covered with olive oil. They had poured the oil all over themselves.

"Watch this," Daddy said with a grin. "Hey, little girls, what do you think you are doing?" he shouted.

The girls being startled tried to get up quickly, but they were slipping and sliding all over the place.

As Daddy and Mommy hid their smiles Daddy said, "Well, I think we had better try to clean up these two little greased pigs, don't you?"

"Yes," said Mother, "I'll take these two little slippery monkeys and you can see if you can clean up this mess, okay?"

"Okay," said Daddy.

"Scrub—a—dub-dub, two little rascals in a tub."

My Fish Can't Pray

Once upon a sunny day in Thackerville, *where it is never right to do wrong and it is never wrong to do right,* a little girl was concerned.

One morning Chelsea's Mommy came into the living room and noticed Chelsea staring intently at her fish in its fishbowl. She had a very worried look on her face.

"What's wrong?" Mommy asked.

"My fish can't pray," Chelsea said sadly.

"Why do you think that your fish can't pray?" Mommy inquired.

"Because he doesn't have knees," said Chelsea. "My Sunday school teacher taught us that we should kneel down beside our beds at night and say our prayers. But my fish doesn't have knees, so, how can he kneel down and say his prayers?"

"Well," explained her Mommy, "God cares for all His little creatures like your fish in a different way. They don't have to kneel and pray He already knows their hearts. We don't have to kneel to pray either," Mother continued, "we have a Heavenly Father that knows our every need, however, He does want to hear from us every day."

"Oh, goodie," said Chelsea with a smile, "maybe my fish and I can pray together sometime."

"Could be Chelsea - could be," Mommy thought with a smile on her face.

Caught in the Act

Once upon a sunny day in Thackerville, *where it is never right to do wrong and it is never wrong to do right,* two little girls were 'caught in the act.'

One evening just before bedtime Mommy heard a strange noise in the kitchen. As she made her way toward the odd noise she had heard, Sarah whisper to her sister Halle a word of caution.

"Hush," Sarah said quietly, "we probably shouldn't eat any of Mommy's cookies before we go to bed."

"I know," whispered Halle, "but they are so good."

Mommy noticed the sound of the lid on the cookie jar clattering. As she peeked around the corner, she saw Halle and Sarah both up on the kitchen counter. Sarah had the cookie jar lid in her hand and was watching her sister with great interest as she stretched deep within the cookie jar to retrieve the ideal cookie.

Mommy rushed quickly to get Daddy. Hiding behind the doorway they watched as the girls carefully chose one cookie after another.

"What do you think we should do?" asked Daddy. "They must be hungry for some of Mommy's yummy cookies. I can't blame them, I am hungry too."

"Well," said Mommy, "I didn't say they couldn't have some cookies."

So, Mommy and Daddy stepped into the kitchen.

"Don't you think that some milk would taste good with these cookies, girls?" Mommy asked.

After that they joined the girls in the raiding of the cookie jar.

The Dancing Bird

Once upon a sunny day in Thackerville, *where it is never right to do wrong and it is never wrong to do right*, two little girls saw a strange sight.

One Saturday morning, while visiting Grandpa and Grandma Thacker's, Cassie and Candy saw a strange white and brown bird dancing in the back yard. Cassie and Candy ran in the house to tell their Grandpa.

"Grandpa!" they shouted excitedly, "come and see the dancing bird. It is brown and white and has a noisy cry."

"A dancing bird?" Grandpa Thacker inquired.

"Yes, Grandpa, come and see!"

So, Grandpa, Candy, and Cassie ran outside to see the dancing bird.

"Oh," said Grandpa, "I see what you mean."

There in the middle of the back yard was a little white and brown bird with its wings lifted and moving back and forth dancing just like the two children had said.

"This bird is called a kildare. She has a nest nearby and she is trying to scare you away so you don't step on her eggs," Grandpa said with a smile. "We just need to stay away so she won't be afraid."

"Okay," said Candy.

"All right," said Cassie, "but can we watch her at a distance, I've never before seen a dancing bird."

"Of course," said Grandpa, "be sure not to get too close."

So, the girls sat on the back porch at a safe distance and watched the odd little bird. They also noticed that every time another bird came near the strange little bird went into her little dance.

CHAPTER 3

ADVENTURES AT GRANDMA'S HOUSE

The Big Egg Hunt

Once upon a sunny day in Thackerville, *where it is never right to do wrong and it is never wrong to do right,* that eight little children went on an egg hunt at Grandpa and Grandma Thacker's house.

One sunny day, Courtney, Candy, Cassie, Cameron, Chelsea, Halle, Sarah and Cody were all excited about the big egg hunt. It had been a family tradition to come to their Grandparent's and Cody's house each year. Grandma always placed little surprises in the plastic eggs so, after they had collected their eggs, they would gather in Grandma's living room, open, and enjoy. Grandma always made sure that everyone enjoyed their meal before the candy was eaten. Grandma would hide the eggs then she always ensured that the smaller children got a head start to be fair. After that head start, the race was on.

"I found a big orange one!" Cameron said excitedly.

"I found a pink one by the big oak tree!" shouted Courtney.

Cassie, Candy and Chelsea ran toward the flagpole where they saw five or six eggs of assorted colors.

"Look at Halle and Sarah everyone!" Grandma shouted.

From nearby the elm trees Halle and Sarah came dragging a big basket between them filled with eggs.

"Now, that is team work," Grandpa said with a chuckle.

All at once the sky opened up and large raindrops began to fall. The egg hunt was over but not before every basket was full.

"What a great day!" the children shouted. Then they all went inside the house to open their treasures.

Hungry Bunnies

Once upon a sunny day in Thackerville, *where it is never right to do wrong and it is never wrong to do right,* that a mystery happened to two little girls.

One day, while at their Grandpa and Grandma Thacker's house, Cassie and Candy were helping plant flowers. After they had finished, they all sat on the front porch and admired all the work that they had accomplished that day.

The next day, Cassie and Candy rushed outside to see all the plants. To their amazement, many of the plants were gone and some others had lost their leaves. They rushed back into the house and called for their Grandma.

"Grandma, Grandma," Cassie shouted!

"What is it girls," Grandma wondered.

"Somebody took our pretty flowers, come and see." Candy said. Grandma went out to the front porch and saw the problem.

"Oh, I see girls, it looks like we have a hungry rabbit problem," she explained.

Just then they glanced in the side yard and there nibbling on a flower was a little gray rabbit.

"Well," said Grandma with a smile, "they are God's little creatures, so, I guess we will have to share our plants with them, okay, girls?"

"Okay," said Cassie.

"Absolutely," agreed Candy, "I'm sure that they won't eat all of them."

She was right. Many plants survived those hungry bunnies.

The Biting Bugs

Once upon a sunny day in Thackerville, *where it is never right to do wrong and it is never wrong to do right,* that a little boy was shocked to find a biting bug.

One day, while visiting his Grandma Thacker, Cameron was playing with Cody in the playground area. Cody was swinging on a swing and Cameron was digging in the sand box. Unexpectedly Cameron jumped up and shouted.

"Cody, Cody!" Cameron said excitedly.

"What is the matter?" Cody questioned.

"Something just bit me," Cameron said.

Cody ran into the house and told Grandma and she came running out with Cody to see what was the matter.

"Show me where you were bit," said Grandma.

Cameron lifted up his arm and showed her a small red bite on his elbow. As Grandma looked at the bite she noticed a little ant crawling away.

"Now I see," said Grandma, "there must be an ant hill in this sand box. You have been digging in his home and he is trying to protect his family. These ants are called soldier ants. They protect the rest from those who would try to hurt them. Maybe you should dig somewhere else," she warned.

"Okay," said Cameron.

"Sure," agreed Cody, "I think we should leave those biting bugs alone."

"Yes," said Cameron, "I have a feeling that there are more soldier ants where that one came from. One bite is enough for me."

God's Little Flashlights

Once upon a sunny day in Thackerville, *where it is never right to do wrong and it is never wrong to do right,* two look-a-like girls and their 'cuncle' saw a wonderful sight.

One evening, Candy and Cassie were at Cody's house, their 'cousin/uncle'. They were playing in the backyard. When all of a sudden they began to see little tiny lights and they were blinking on and off all over the yard. They saw one, and then two, and before long, they were all around them.

"Cody!" shouted Cassie, "go tell Grandma Thacker."

"Okay," said Cody.

Cody ran inside the house and found his Mommy.

"Mommy, Mommy," he shouted, "there are hundreds of little flashlights in our backyard!"

"Flashlights?" inquired Mommy.

"Yes," said Cody excitedly, "come and see!"

Mommy rushed outside with Cody and sure enough the night was filled with little blinking lights.

"Oh," said Mommy, "I see what you mean. These little bugs are called lightning bugs. God created them that way. They sure bring beauty to the night. Aren't they pretty?"

"Oh, yes, Grandma!" Candy said with a big smile on her face.

Cassie grinned and said, "I'll just call them God's little flashlights."

"Okay, Cassie Jo." said Grandma, "God would like that."

"Can we catch them and put them in a jar, Grandma?" asked Candy.

"I guess so, Candy girl, but you need to put holes in the lid so they can breathe and then release them later, okay?"

"All right," they all promised.

So, they ran all around the backyard gathering God's little flashlights.

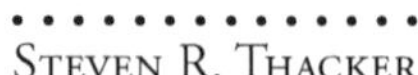

The Parachutist

Once upon a sunny day in Thackerville, *where it is never right to do wrong and it is never wrong to do right,* a little boy tried something new.

One sunny morning Cody decided to try something that he had seen on television the night before. He had been watching an old war movie with his Daddy about some soldiers parachuting behind the enemy lines. So, Cody had a great idea. He went into the closet and got out the big umbrella and headed to the barn.

On his way out the door his Mother asks him, "Cody, where are you going with that umbrella?"

"I'm going to war, Mommy!" he said excitedly.

"What does he mean by that statement?" Daddy asks.

"I don't really know," Mommy said with a questioned look on her face.

"Well," Daddy pondered, "last night we were watching a war movie about soldiers parachuting behind enemy lines. Maybe it has something to do with that."

"Oh, no!" Mommy exclaimed, "he had a big umbrella in his hand. You don't think that he would try to jump off some building, do you?"

Father and Mother looked at each other and shouted in unison, "The Barn!"

As they rushed out the door they were just in time to see Cody with umbrella in both hands screaming, "Geronimo!"

Seconds later he hit the ground with a thud and rolled into the weeds.

They rushed to him and ask him if he was alright.

"I'm just fine, Mommy, but it sure looked easier on television."

The Best Dinner Ever

Once upon a sunny day in Thackerville, *where it is never right to do wrong and it is never wrong to do right,* a dinner was enjoyed.

One day Grandma Steiner came to Corey and Shawn's house to fix a spaghetti dinner. They helped her carry into the house the grocery bags because she always cooked from 'scratch'.

The two little boys were nosey as they helped her empty the bags onto the kitchen table.

"What is this?" Corey asked as he held up a container for Grandma Steiner to see.

"That is bay leaf," she answered, "it is an herb for the spaghetti sauce."

"It looks like a dead leaf from off one of our bushes outside," said Shawn. "Do we really eat it?"

"No, I put it in the sauce to flavor it and when it has finished cooking I will take it out," Grandma said with a chuckle.

The sauce took a long time to cook so Grandma and Mommy visited while the boys went to their room to play for a while.

The dinner was done just in time for Daddy to come home from work.

As they sat at the kitchen table Daddy thanked God for the food then they all took turns telling about what they did that day.

After dinner everyone helped clean and put away the dishes.

"Now for dessert," said Grandma Steiner with a grin, "I brought my homemade chocolate candies."

"Did you bring my favorite caramel-pecan turtles?" Shawn asked with joy.

"What about my favorite buckeyes," interrupted Corey?

"Yes, I made them and more for us all to enjoy," Grandma said proudly.

They all enjoyed the homemade candies and each other that evening.

Steven R. Thacker

Two Boys Faced with a Problem

Once upon a sunny day in Thackerville, *where it is never right to do wrong and it is never wrong to do right,* two little boys were faced with a problem.

One sunny day as Cameron and Cody were playing in the back yard at Grandpa and Grandma Thacker's, Cameron got an idea. "Let's get Grandpa's golf cart and carry some boards over to the playground to build a fort," Cameron said.

"Okay," Cody said, "it will make it easier to carry the boards, but shouldn't we ask permission first?"

"No," said Cameron, "Grandpa isn't home and I'm sure he won't mind."

"Okay," said Cody.

So, the boys loaded the wood onto the golf cart, drove it to the playground and built their fort. But just as they were putting the golf cart back they bumped into the corner of the garage and put a little dent in it.

"Oh, no!" shouted Cody, "now what are we going to do?"

"Well," said Cameron, "we need to tell Grandma."

"But it is not a very big dent," said Cody.

"Yes, but as Grandpa always says it is never right to do wrong and it is never wrong to do right," said Cameron.

"Yes," said Cody, "I guess you're right, let's go."

So, the two little boys went into the house and told Grandma all that had happened.

"I'm not angry," said Grandma, "but I am disappointed that you didn't come to me first. You need to remember something boys."

"What's that?" they asked.

"Dents in a garage can be fixed," Grandma said, "but dishonesty can hurt for a lifetime."

THE LITTLE GREEN APPLES

Once upon a sunny day in Thackerville, *where it is never right to do wrong and it is never wrong to do right,* two little boys learned a valuable lesson.

One afternoon at Grandma Thacker's house, Cody and Cameron decided to go down over the hill to eat some of Grandma's apples. Grandma had told them that they were green and that they may make them sick. Disregarding Grandma's warning the boys headed to the apple tree.

Once there they climbed the tree and began to enjoy the apples. Soon Cameron notice that Cody was sitting on a limb all slumped over.

"What's wrong, Cody?" Cameron asked.

"Oh, Cameron, I feel sick," said Cody with a groan.

"I feel kind of sick myself," Cameron said.

So the boys ran back to Grandma's house.

"Grandma," they whimpered, "we don't feel very good."

"Have you two been in my apple tree eating those little green apples?" Grandma inquired.

"Yes, we have but we thought that a few little apples wouldn't hurt," Cody said.

"Sometimes disobedience will cost you something," Grandma said with a smile, "and this time it will cost in a stomach ache and the castor oil that you're both going to have to take to get over it."

"Oh no!" said the boys with a groan, "we are so sorry."

The Spooky Fur

Once upon a sunny day in Thackerville, *where it is never right to do wrong and it is never wrong to do right,* two little girls saw a mystery.

One day, at their Grandpa and Grandma Thacker's, Cassie and Candy were out in the backyard playing in the playground when Candy noticed a little pile of gray fur in the yard.

"Cassie!" Candy shouted.

"What is it?" Cassie questioned.

"Look at that little mound of fur? Let's go and see what it is!"

"Okay," said Cassie.

So, the two girls ran to the pile of fur. Just as they were bending over it for a closer look, it moved. The frightened girls ran as fast as they could for the house.

"Grandpa, Grandpa," they shouted, "come and see the spooky fur!"

"Spooky fur?" Grandpa questioned.

"Yes," said Cassie, "come with us."

They took Grandpa by the hand and ran to the mysterious pile of fur.

"See, Grandpa," said Candy, "it moves and there is no body."

Grandpa leaned over and moved the fur back slowly and said in a quiet voice, "Look, girls."

Under the pile of fur were four little bunnies all cuddled together.

"Oh, they are so cute," said Cassie sweetly. "Can we hold them?"

"No," said Grandpa, "their Mommy will return soon and we must not disturb them."

Later that day, the girls saw the Mommy rabbit come cautiously back to her babies. The mystery of the pile of spooky fur was solved.

A Kite with Legs

Once upon a sunny day in Thackerville, *where it is never right to do wrong and it is never wrong to do right,* two little girls seen a kite that had legs.

One day, while playing in their Grandpa and Grandma Thacker's back yard, Sarah and Halle saw a strange little bug flying slowly. They went to tell their Grandpa.

"Grandpa," said Halle, "come and see these odd little bugs that have been flying around us."

"Yes, Grandpa, come see!" added Sarah. "Are they stinging bugs?" she questioned.

"Well," said Grandpa, "let's go and have a look-see."

So, Grandpa and the two girls went to see the strange bugs.

"See, Grandpa!" said Halle excitedly, "they are still here."

"Do they have stingers, Grandpa?" asked Sarah.

"No," Grandpa said with a smile, "this is called a June bug. They won't hurt you, but they can be fun."

Grandpa reached into his pocket and pulled out a short length of string. He caught one of the June bugs and carefully tied one end of the string to one of its legs.

"Now, watch," he said, as he turned the bug loose. It flew slowly around Grandpa's head.

"That is the cleverest thing that I have ever seen," said Halle.

"Yes," said Sarah, "I've never seen a kite with legs before."

"Just remember, girls," added Grandpa, "this is one of God's little creatures and you should be very careful not to hurt it. Just let it go after a little while."

"Okay," said the girls, as they flew their new kite with legs.

CHAPTER 4

AROUND THACKERVILLE

THE SAND TRAP

Once upon a sunny day in Thackerville, *where it is never right to do wrong and it is never wrong to do right,* a little boy was trapped with no help from his dog, Neko.

One day, as he went outside to play, Cody was reminded by his Mommy that he would need to come back inside in about an hour for lunch. Later, when it was time for lunch, Mommy notices that Cody had not returned.

"Cody," Mommy called, "it's time for lunch."

She just thought that he simply had lost track of time. But Cody did not come in. So, Mommy called a second time.

"Cody," Mommy called again. Still there was no Cody.

"Mommy," Daddy called, "come to the window."

As Mommy looked out of the window she saw the reason that Cody was unable to come in. There in his sandbox was Cody covered up to his armpits with sand. So, Mommy and Daddy rushed out to see if he was alright.

"Are you trapped son?" Mommy asked.

"I sure am," said Cody, "and Neko is no help at all."

So, Daddy and Mommy dug him out and led him directly to the shower.

Later Cody asked Daddy a question.

"Daddy," Cody questioned, "is this the kind of sand trap problem that you have on the golf course?"

"No," said Daddy with a chuckle, "we generally try to stay 'on top' of the sand when we play golf and not under it."

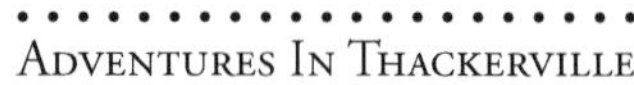

A Fort was Built

Once upon a sunny day in Thackerville, *where it is never right to do wrong and it is never wrong to do right*, that a little boy went to war.

One winter day as the sun was shining and the snow was falling, Cody took his big American flag that his Daddy had given him that used to hang on the front porch and went out into the snow to go to war. Soon his Mommy came outside and asks him a question.

"Cody," she asked, "do you want to build a fort for your soldiers to fight in?"

"Yes!" exclaimed Cody, "that's a great idea."

So, they began to gather large snowballs to build the walls. Cody's dog, Melvin, tried to help but only made matters worse. Soon, the walls were complete and ready for battle.

"Now," said Cody, "I can fight the enemy."

"You sure can," said Mommy with a big smile on her face.

And all of a sudden, Cody was being bombarded with a hail of snowballs from Mommy. Soon, the air was filled with snowballs going back and forth.

All at once Mommy shouted, "I surrender! Why don't we sign a peace agreement and celebrate with a cup of hot chocolate?"

"Sounds good to me," said Cody as he shook off the snow.

The Hunter

Once upon a sunny day in Thackerville, *where it is never right to do wrong and it is never wrong to do right,* a little boy saw a curious sight.

One day after he had finished eating lunch, Cody went outside to see how Mommy's garden was doing with his dog, Neko. As he ran toward the garden he noticed that, Princess, Mommy's cat was acting very strange.

"Look at Princess," said Cody to Neko, "look how she is standing very, very still?"

"Maybe she is hurt," Cody thought out loud, "I'll go and tell Mommy."

So, Cody ran inside the house and brought Mommy out to see the motionless cat.

"See," said Cody, "something is wrong with Princess."

"No," said Mommy with a smile, "there is nothing wrong with Princess. Come with me and I'll show you what is going on."

So, Mommy took Cody by the hand and quietly led him to the old oak tree in the back yard. There on a lower limb was a robin's nest with three little babies in it. They were calling for their mother.

"Cats are hunters by nature," said Mommy, "and if we do not discourage Princess from this nest she may hurt these babies. So, the next time you see Princess acting like that just chase her away, okay?"

"Okay," said Cody.

The rest of the day Cody and Neko kept a close eye on Princess and the robin's nest.

The Invaders

Once upon a sunny day in Thackerville, *where it is never right to do wrong and it is never wrong to do right,* Daddy saw something strange.

One morning Daddy was loading some mulch into a small trailer to place around the flowers. Suddenly, a swarm of bees flew over his head. There seemed to be thousands of them and in just a matter of a few seconds they were gone. The next morning, as he went back outside to finish working, he noticed a strange ball shaped object hanging on the lilac bush. He ran back inside the house to tell Chelsea.

"Come outside with me!" Daddy said excitedly.

Once outside, he explained that these were honey bees.

"Why are they here?" Chelsea questioned.

"I don't know," answered Daddy, "for some reason the queen bee decided to leave her hive and go searching for a new home and she chose our lilac bush."

"What do we do now?" asked Chelsea. "Will they sting us?"

"Perhaps, so you must stay away from them," Daddy warned.

Daddy called a man he knew who had bee hives. The next day the 'Bee Hive' man came with a big white box.

"What is that?" Chelsea asked.

"It will be our invaders new home," said Daddy.

They watched as the man took the new bee hive and set it under the limb where the bees were hanging and gently shook them into the box. Soon they were all safely inside their new home.

Cody Makes a Friend

Once upon a sunny day in Thackerville, *where it is never right to do wrong and it is never wrong to do right,* Cody surprised his Daddy.

One morning Cody and his Daddy were working in the flower area around the flag pole. Daddy warned Cody to be very quiet because the mommy robin was on the nest near where they were working. "Do you think that I could hold the baby birds like I did the baby rabbits?" Cody asked.

"No," answered Daddy, "the momma bird might peck you to keep you from hurting her babies."

As Daddy continued to work in the flower bed he noticed that Cody was over by the robin's nest.

"What are you doing?" questioned his Daddy.

"I'm petting the momma robin," answered Cody.

"Petting the robin?" asked Daddy in surprise!

"Yes, Daddy," answered Cody, "she doesn't seem to mind at all."

"She must feel that you mean them no harm," said Daddy. "Birds have a special sense when things are safe. God has made them in a very special way."

"I'm glad," said Cody with a smile, "I like birds."

"Yes," said Daddy, "me too."

Daddy's Big Helper

Once upon a sunny day in Thackerville, *where it is never right to do wrong and it is never wrong to do right,* Daddy had a big helper.

One sunny Saturday morning, Daddy had a big job to do in the yard.

"May I help?" asked Courtney.

"Yes, you may," answer Daddy, "but it will be a big job and will take most of the day. I thought that you had plans to play with your friends."

"I did," answered Courtney, "but the Bible says that I should honor my Father and Mother and I feel that by my being your helper, I will show Jesus that I honor you. Besides, it would not be very nice for me to go and play and not help."

"Okay," said Daddy with a smile, "I would love to have your help."

So, Courtney carried the bricks for her Daddy while he crawled along the ground around the flower beds and placed them in just the right spot. When the job was finished they stood back and admired their work.

"It sure looks good doesn't it, Daddy?" questioned Courtney proudly.

"It sure does," answer Daddy, "but I could not have done it without my big helper."

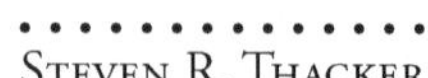

The Black Squirrel

Once upon a sunny day in Thackerville, *where it is never right to do wrong and it is never wrong to do right,* a little boy saw a strange thing.

One day as Cameron went to Great Grandma and Grandpa Speakman's house in Jamestown, Ohio, he noticed a very strange, little animal. Grandpa had given Daddy an air compressor and Daddy had borrowed someone's pick-up truck to bring it home in. As Cameron and his Daddy were driving down the alley next to Grandpa's house, Cameron shouted, "Daddy, look, there's a little black squirrel on that telephone wire!"

Daddy stopped the truck to see but the little squirrel was gone.

"What do you think you saw?" questioned Daddy.

"It was a black squirrel!" Cameron said excitedly.

"A black squirrel?" Daddy questioned with a chuckle.

"Yes, Daddy, I'm sure it was a squirrel," said Cameron.

"Well," said Daddy, "I've never seen a black squirrel. I think that you may have been mistaken."

Later, Cameron looked up on top of the garage and there, as if to tease him, was that same little squirrel. He shouted at Daddy to look but it again was too late, the squirrel disappeared up a tree.

Soon, the truck was loaded. As Cameron and his Daddy were driving slowly down the driveway there on a lower branch of a tree was that pesky little black squirrel with a big nut in its mouth, and looking straight at Daddy.

"Well, well, well," said Daddy, "I guess black squirrels do exist after all. I'm so sorry, son, that I doubted you," said Daddy.

"Oh, that's alright, Daddy. I'm just glad that the mystery is solved," said Cameron.

Daddy's Big Catch.

Once upon a sunny day in Thackerville, *where it is never right to do wrong and it is never wrong to do right,* Daddy caught a critter.

One day as Halle and Sarah returned home from a long journey with their Daddy and Mommy, Daddy went out to check the chickens. After making sure that they were safe, he went up near the house where he had set a cage trap to catch any nosey coons that might have been snooping around. As he came near the cage, he noticed that instead of a coon in his cage, he had trapped a skunk. He ran in and called for Halle, Sarah and Mommy to come quickly and see the critter that he had mistakenly caught in his trap. As they slipped quietly out towards the cage, and noticed that the little black animal had a big white stripe on its back.

"Oh, Daddy," said Halle, "that's a skunk!"

"Yes," said Sarah, "but it is asleep. Should we wake it?"

"No, no, no!" cautioned Daddy, "but I have an idea."

So, everyone tip-toed quickly and quietly back into the house.

"Now, great white hunter," said Mommy with a laugh, "what are you going to do with your little critter?"

"Well," said Daddy with a smile, "you'll see."

So, Daddy took a large blanket and he carefully and quietly covered the cage and then gently carried it over the hill to the edge of the big woods. He then took a long stick and gently opened the cage door and moved away at a safe distance.

Then the little skunk went back into the woods.

"Maybe the next time," Mommy said with a smile, "you should place a sign on the cage saying 'no skunks allowed'."

Patches' New Friend

Once upon a sunny day in Thackerville, *where it is never right to do wrong and it is never wrong to do right,* Patches found a reluctant new friend.

One evening, as Halle and Sarah was returning from church with their parents, they noticed their dog, Patches, acting strange. Patches was barking wildly at something up the old oak tree in their front yard.

"What do you think Patches is barking at?" ask Sarah.

"I don't know, Sarah," Daddy said, "but as soon as everyone is safely in the house, I will go and see."

After everyone was safe inside, Daddy took the flashlight outside to investigate.

Soon, Daddy returned with Patches and said, "Keep this crazy dog in the house."

"Okay," said Mommy, "we will, but what is going on?"

"Well," said Daddy with a smile, "it seems that our dog is trying to make a new friend and the other animal wants nothing to do with Patches. It seems that our dog has treed a groundhog."

So, Daddy took a long stick and gently persuaded the groundhog to leave the tree and it scampered into the woods.

"I guess Patches will have to find another friend, right, Daddy?" said Halle with a smile.

"Yes," said Daddy with a chuckle, "but maybe the next friend needs to be less dangerous, like a squirrel."

The Jar with Legs

Once upon a sunny day in Thackerville, *where it is never right to do wrong and it is never wrong to do right,* two little girls saw something odd.

Candy and Cassie were returning home with their Daddy and Mommy from the store and they saw something strange go across their driveway into their back yard.

"Did you see that?" shouted Mommy!

"I sure did!" said Daddy.

"It looked like a big white jar with legs," said Candy.

"Yes, I saw it too," said Cassie excitedly, "and it sure was in a hurry!"

"Well," said Daddy, "just as soon as everyone is safely inside the house I will go and try to solve the mystery."

So, as soon as everyone was safe inside, Daddy took his flashlight and went back outside. Soon, Daddy returned and was laughing so hard that he could hardly speak.

"What is so funny?" asked Mommy.

"Yes, Daddy, did you find the big jar with legs?" chimed in the girls.

"I sure did," said Daddy, "come and see."

Out in the back corner of the backyard they saw a small dog with his head stuck inside a large plastic jar.

"How did he get into this kind of a fix?" asked Candy.

"Well," said Daddy with a smile, "I guess his curiosity just got the best of him."

Then, Daddy carefully and gently freed the little nosey nuisance. As soon as the curious canine was freed he dashed back across the yard and headed for home.

Chapter 5

Long, Long Ago

The Highwayman

Once upon a sunny day in Thackerville, *where it is never right to do wrong and it is never wrong to do right,* many years ago, Great Grandpa and Grandma Weaver went on a journey.

A long, long, long time ago Great Grandpa and Grandma Weaver decided to go to town. Grandpa went into the barn to prepare, Old Mert, Grandpa's mule for the journey. As he hitched him up to the wagon he heard Grandma call. "Are you about ready, Pa?" Grandma shouted!

"Yes, I am, Ma." Grandpa assured her.

Soon, she saw Old Mert coming out of the barn with Grandpa on the buckboard, and ready to go to town. As soon as Grandma climbed on board, they headed for town. The clop, clop, clop of Mert's hoofs could be heard echoing through the woods on that crisp clear morning. Just then they noticed a strange man standing, rather suspiciously, along the side of the road ahead.

"What do you think he wants, Pa?" Grandma asked nervously.

"I don't know," answered Grandpa, "but I'm ready for him."

As they neared the stranger, they noticed that he was holding a gun.

"He's a highwayman!" shouted Grandpa, "hang on!"

With a crack of the whip to the back of Old Mert they were off at a full gallop. Just as they passed the highwayman Grandpa gave a couple of lashes toward him for good measure.

Soon Grandpa slowed Mert down to a gentle walk.

"Well, do you think we are safe now, Pa?" Grandma asked.

"Yes, I do," Grandpa said proudly, "but just in case, I will keep my whip handy."

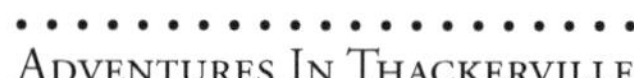

Grandma's Bible

Once upon a sunny day in Thackerville, *where it is never right to do wrong and it is never wrong to do right,* Grandpa Thacker shared a memory of years ago.

As the grandchildren circled all around, Grandpa told a story. As a child, (very long ago) his Grandmother's Bible was a central figure in her home. There were many times that he found her reading and studying the words written therein. Grandma Weaver would tell of the many heroes' of the faith like, Gideon, David, Moses and Joshua, to mention just a few. She would often encourage him to follow the godly examples that were written in her Bible. One day he ask her why her Bible was so important to her.

"Well, Steve," Grandma said with a smile, "this Bible helps me to know God's will for my life."

"How does the Bible do that?" Steve asked.

"God guides me to certain passages of scripture that will give me the peace that I am in need of," she said.

Grandma continued, "But there is another special part of this wonderful book."

"What is that?" asked Steve.

"It has the record of our family written in it."

She opened to the front of her Bible and there was listed all the names of her children and their families with birthdates and special events, even the date of her and Grandpa's marriage.

"Wow, Grandma!" Steve said excitedly, "now I understand why your Bible is so special to you."

"Yes, this Book is very special," Grandma said with a smile.

The Bear Cave

Once upon a sunny day in Thackerville, *where it is never right to do wrong and it is never wrong to do right,* many years ago a little boy went on an adventure.

One bright and sunny morning little Steve decided to go deep within Grandma's woods to see the big rocks. He took a sack with a sandwich and two cookies in it. He also took his canteen full of water.

Soon, he and his faithful dog, Brownie, were on their way. Grandma had warned him of the many animals that were in the woods and how he should be very careful. So, armed with his slingshot in his back pocket and five pebbles he was sure that he was well able to face any dangers that would come along.

As they journeyed deeper and deeper into the woods he soon came to a stream flowing over a big cliff. As he made his way around the side of the cliff he saw a large opening under the waterfall.

"Hey, Brownie!" Steve said excitedly, "look at this big area under the waterfall."

Just then he noticed a large hole in the back of the cave.

"This must be a bear's cave," said Steve in a whisper.

All of a sudden he heard a noise of something moving through the bushes behind him.

Brownie began to growl.

"I think that we had better head for home," Steve said nervously.

He and Brownie both scampered for home.

As they ran Steve said to Brownie, "I think that we can hunt for bears another day, don't you?"

"Me too," answered Brownie with a 'big bark'!

GRANDMA'S CURE

Once upon a sunny day in Thackerville, *where it is never right to do wrong and it is never wrong to do right*, many years ago three little boys needed Grandma's help.

One sunny but cold Saturday morning in January, Steve, Neil, and Gary decided that they were going to go sledding.

"Be aware," Grandma warned, "the cold can strike very quick and you have a very long way to walk to return home."

"Don't worry, Grandma," Steve said with a smile. "We're experienced," he said proudly, "we've done this before."

"Yes, I know you have but today is different. It's going to get very cold, very fast," she warned, "so, be careful, okay?"

"Okay!" shouted the boys as they rushed out into the snow.

Grandma watched as the three little boys crossed the big field pulling their sleds behind them.

After about two hours of sledding Neil shouted to Gary, "I can hardly feel my fingers! We need to be heading back."

"Yes," said Steve, "Grandma warned us about the cold."

Soon the boys were headed back but the snow had begun to blow very hard and the wind was colder than before.

Finally, they arrived at Grandma's house all covered with snow and about frozen.

Then they noticed Grandma do an odd thing.

"Okay, boys," Grandma said sternly, "sit here around the stove and put your hands in this pan of cold water."

"Cold water?" the boys exclaimed!

"Yes, boys," she assured them, "your Grandma knows best."
Sure enough the boys were soon nice and warm again and ready to go back outside.

The Feather Tick Mattress

Once upon a sunny day in Thackerville, *where it is never right to do wrong and it is never wrong to do right,* many years ago, two little boys went to Great Grandma's house.

Corey and Shawn loved to go to Great Grandma Weaver's house. It was a long drive south of their home.

"Oh boy!" shouted Corey. "I love to go to Grandma's."

"Yes," said Shawn, "there is always so much to do."

"Well, children, we're almost at Grandma's house. Just a couple more miles," said Father. "What will you do first?"

"Well," said Shawn with a smile, "I guess my favorite part of going to Grandma's is Grandma herself. I'm going to give her a big hug."

"Yes," said Corey in agreement, "she knows everything. I love to hear her tell about the old days when she raised her children during the great depression after your Grandpa died."

"You are right, boys. She's quite a lady," Daddy said proudly.

"I guess one of the best things about Grandma's house is that big old feather bed we get to sleep on," said Corey smiling.

"Yes," agreed Shawn, "it's HUGE and I bet the whole family could sleep on that thing."

"Well, boys, I've got a secret to tell you about that big old feather tick mattress," said Daddy with a smile.

"What's that, Daddy?" asked the boys.

"I enjoyed sleeping on that same mattress when I was your age. I remember in the winter time how Grandma would take a smooth stone from off the top of stove and wrap it in a towel then place it at the foot of my bed under the covers. That rock would keep me toasty warm all night. Yes, I also love that old feather bed."

Grandma's Roofing Job

Once upon a sunny day in Thackerville, *where it is never right to do wrong and it is never wrong to do right,* Grandma fixed her roof.

Grandma Weaver was never one to ask for help when a job had to be done. Although Grandma was now well up into her eighties she still insisted on doing things on her own.

"What are you doing?" ask Steve.

"Well," Grandma said in a whisper, "I plan on going up on the porch roof and fix some of those old shingles that are loose."

"Now, Grandma," Steve warned, "you know that you should not be going up that old ladder. You might fall and hurt yourself. Instead, why don't we ask someone to help?"

"No sir, little boy," said Grandma sternly, "I have been climbing ladders and fixing roofs long before you were born."

And with that she tied on a little nail apron with a hammer and some nails in it then grabbed a few shingles and headed up the ladder. After about an hour she came down all sweaty and tired. Just as she neared the bottom of the ladder she slipped and fell to the ground with a thud. Grandma ended up in a nearby bush.

Steve ran over to help her up. "Are you alright, Grandma?" Steve asks trembling.

"The only thing I hurt was my pride," said Grandma with a chuckle.

"Okay, Grandma," Steve said, "but the next time let's get help, okay?"

"Okay," Grandma promised as she climbed out of the bush.

The Pop Bottle Hunt

Once upon a sunny day in Thackerville, *where it is never right to do wrong and it is never wrong to do right,* two little boy's made a mistake.

"Hey, Steve!" Neil said excitedly, "I've got a great idea!"

"What is it, Neil?" Steve asks.

"How would you like some candy?" Neil probed.

"Oh, that would be wonderful," Steve said with a big laugh, "but what are we going to use for money?"

"Well," said Neil, "I've been thinking on that very problem and I think I have a solution."

"Yeah," said Steve, "what is it?"

"I was looking in our garage and found five pop bottles and I am sure that as we walk all the way to the store we will find some others."

"Hey, that's a great idea!" Steve said with a shout, "and I remember seeing three bottles on my back porch."

So, the two little boys began their journey, searching the ditches all along the way to the country store. As they found a bottle they would be careful to clean it up real good because the man at the store said he would not accept any dirty bottles.

Soon, their little wagon was filled with pop bottles and the boys were excitedly counting all the money that they would make. They finally arrived at the store. That is when they noticed a big 'closed' sign on the door.

"Oh, no," Neil shouted, "today is Sunday!"

"Well," said Steve with a chuckle, "I'm sure that all that candy will still be there tomorrow and maybe we can find more bottles."

So, the two tired little boys turned their little wagon around and headed for home disappointed but not defeated.

The Adventure

Once upon a sunny day in Thackerville, *where it is never right to do wrong and it is never wrong to do right*, a young boy had an adventure.

Steve was visiting his cousin's home and stayed all day. They played in the big woods behind the house where the Lord of creation had provided rocks to climb, a big willow tree to swing from and caves to explore. But one place was more special than them all. They loved to play down at the big rocks. The children would play there for hours and hours. They would climb the big rock and pretend that they were on a Pirate Ship in the middle of the ocean, or at Fort Sumter where the first shot was fired in the Civil War, or perhaps they were on a high mountain looking for buried treasure. Yes, going to the big rocks was a great adventure. But as with all adventures their time was getting short and it was time for Steve to be heading home.

"Oh, Rodney," said Steve, "what a wonderful day this has been."

"Well, let's get together again very soon," said Rodney.

"Oh, yes, I would like that very much," Steve said with a smile. And with that he made his way home.

As he neared Grandma's house he could see smoke coming from the chimney. Grandma was at the old cook stove making supper when he came in and she questioned, "Well, son, did you have a good day?"

"Oh, yes, Grandma," Steve said with a smile, "we had a wonderful day! But, Grandma, do you know what the best time is?"

"What is that, honey?" Grandma asks.

"Coming home," he said. "Coming home to my Grandma."

The Train Man

Once upon a sunny day in Thackerville, *where it is never right to do wrong and it is never wrong to do right*, four little children got a big surprise from the man in the big engine.

One day as Pat, David, Greg, and Steve were playing on the old willow tree out in front of the house. They loved to swing back and forth across the wide ditch next to the railroad tracks.

When they heard the big train coming down the track, the children loved to sit on the bank and watch the big black train as it came huffing and puffing down the track every day. There was a nice man in the front of the train and he always waved at them and tooted the loud horn.

Today seemed different somehow as the big train began to slow down near their house instead of racing by. As the big train got closer and closer they could see the man's face clearly. He had a big smile on his face. The train came to a stop. The man looked out his window and spoke to the children.

"How are you children doing today?" he asks.

"Just fine," said David with a puzzled look on his face.

"Well," continued the man, "I always enjoy seeing you kids every day and I thought that today I would stop and say thank you and give you a little present."

He then reached back into his little room, brought out a box, and lowered it down to the ground. He then climbed back into his seat and started the big train forward again. Soon he was out of sight.

In the box the children found four bottles of pop and four candy bars. What a wonderful surprise! The children rarely ever saw such wonderful treats. They took the box over under the willow tree and had a picnic and talked about the nice man in the big black train.

The Penny Toss

Once upon a sunny day in Thackerville, *where it is never right to do wrong and it is never wrong to do right,* some children were surprise.

One day, while the grandchildren were at Grandma and Grandpa Thacker's home, Grandpa told them a story.

"Many years ago when I was just a boy," Grandpa explained, "I and several other children in the neighborhood were surprised by my Uncle Leonard. He called us all out to my Grandma Weaver's big driveway and had us to all line up. He then took out a large bag of pennies from his old coat pocket."

"Okay, children!" he shouted. "Let's have a penny chase."

And with a quick fling of his hands he threw the pennies out into Grandma's gravel and dirt driveway. We rushed out to gather as many as we could. After about five minutes we came back with all the pennies that we could find.

Just then he shouted again, "Look, children, I have more!"

With another flick of his hand he tossed another handful of pennies into the driveway.

"What a wonderful day it was," Grandpa continued. "After we had gathered all the pennies that we could find Uncle Leonard loaded us all up in his old pickup truck. He took us to the store where we could spend our pennies. For years following that day we would still find a stray penny that had escaped the probing eyes of those little children so many years before."